P9-DWF-023

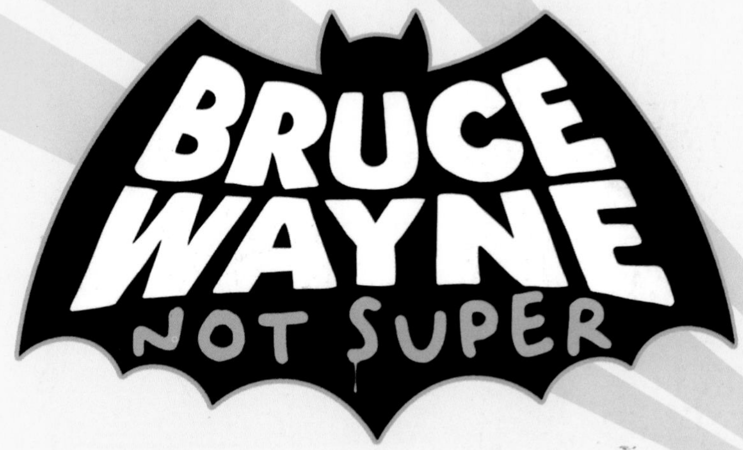
BRUCE
WAYNE
NOT SUPER

Written by

Stuart Gibbs

Art by

Berat Pekmezci

Letters by

Taylor Esposito

BATMAN created by
BOB KANE with BILL FINGER

SUPERMAN created by
JERRY SIEGEL and JOE SHUSTER
By special arrangement with
the JERRY SIEGEL family

Jim Chadwick Editor
Courtney Jordan Associate Editor
Steve Cook Design Director - Books
Amie Brockway-Metcalf Publication Design
Tiffany Huang Publication Production

Marie Javins Editor-in-Chief, DC Comics

Anne DePies Senior VP - General Manager
Jim Lee Publisher & Chief Creative Officer
Don Falletti VP - Manufacturing Operations & Workflow Management
Lawrence Ganem VP - Talent Services
Alison Gill Senior VP - Manufacturing & Operations
Jeffrey Kaufman VP - Editorial Strategy & Programming
Nick J. Napolitano VP - Manufacturing Administration & Design
Nancy Spears VP - Revenue

BRUCE WAYNE: NOT SUPER

DC Comics, 4000 Warner Blvd., Bldg. 700, 2nd Floor, Burbank, CA 91522
Printed by Worzalla, Stevens Point, WI, USA. 1/27/23.
First printing.
ISBN: 978-1-77950-767-9

Library of Congress Cataloging-in-Publication Data

Names: Gibbs, Stuart, 1969- author. | Pekmezci, Berat, 1986- artist. | Esposito, Taylor, letterer.
Title: Bruce Wayne : not super / written by Stuart Gibbs ; art by Berat Pekmezci ; letters by Taylor Esposito.
Description: Burbank, CA : DC Comics, [2023] | "Batman created by Bob Kane with Bill Finger - Superman created by Jerry Siegel and Joe Shuster. By special arrangement with the Jerry Siegel family" | Audience: Ages 8-12 | Audience: Grades 4-6 | Summary: Bruce Wayne, the only kid in school without super powers, gets called to the principal because his career choice of vigilantism is deemed too ambitious, and he becomes even more determined to prove he belongs.
Identifiers: LCCN 2022045294 | ISBN 9781779507679 (trade paperback)
Subjects: CYAC: Identity--Fiction. | Belonging--Fiction. | Superheroes--Fiction. | Gotham City (Imaginary place)--Fiction. | Graphic novels. | LCGFT: Graphic novels.
Classification: LCC PZ7.7.G5324 Br 2023 | DDC 741.5/973--dc23/eng/20221017
LC record available at https://lccn.loc.gov/2022045294

For Violet and Dashiell.
—Stuart

For my wife, Gökçe.
—Berat

TABLE OF CONTENTS

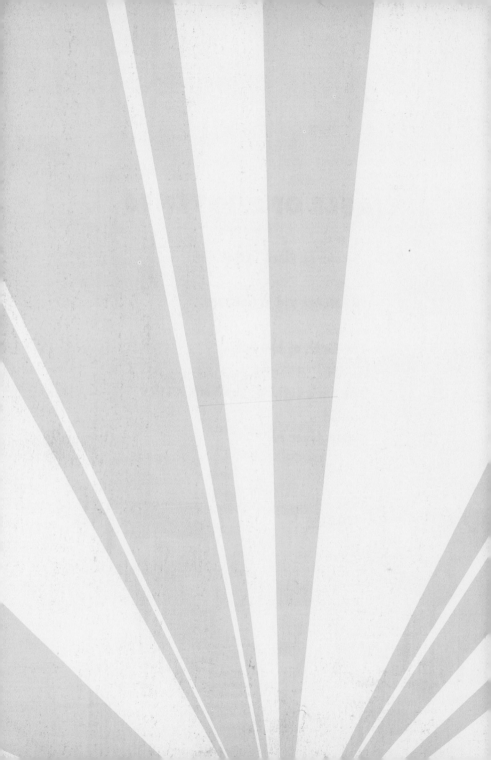

Chapter 1: The Worst Place in Gotham

There's a lot of competition for what the worst place in Gotham is. Like Crime Alley here...

Or Blackgate Penitentiary...
BLACKGATE PENITENTIARY
GCPD

Or Slaughter Swamp...

Or Arkham Asylum.
ARKHAM ASYLUM
But even all these places pale in comparison to the **absolute** worst place in Gotham...

My middle school.
GOTHAM PREPARATORY SCHOOL FOR THE REALLY REALLY GIFTED
All right, I'll admit, it doesn't **look** terrible. But trust me, it **is.**
For **me,** at least.

My name's Bruce. Bruce Wayne. And I don't really fit in here.

That's me on the right. The only kid at this school who doesn't look like they should be a professional leotard model.

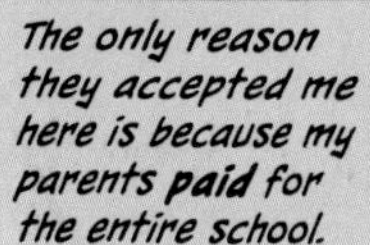
The only reason they accepted me here is because my parents **paid** for the entire school.

W
The students and faculty of Gotham Prep are indebted to Thomas and Martha Wayne, whose great generosity made the construction of this school possible.

My folks were the richest people in town. They made this huge donation to the city to fund Gotham Prep shortly before...
Well, before they were killed by a mugger in Crime Alley.

Of course, it was against the official rules to allow a kid without powers to attend Gotham Prep, but no one balked at letting me in.

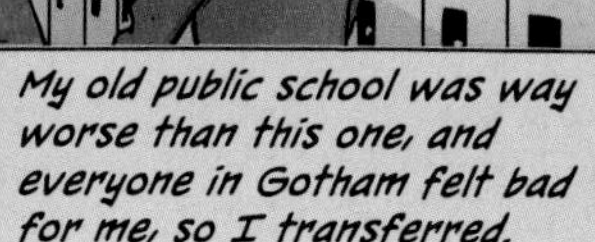
My old public school was way worse than this one, and everyone in Gotham felt bad for me, so I transferred.

Not all of the other kids' powers are amazing.
No one else has the super-strength of Clark Kent.
Oops! Dang it! Not again!
PLOINK
Look out! I'm late to class!
Or the super-speed of Barry Allen.
WHOOSH
Or the grace and dexterity of Diana Prince.
Aaaah!
THUMP
Sorry!
Some of the powers are kind of meh...
Like Arthur Curry's ability to communicate with fish.
BIOLOGY CLASS
What's that guys?
...You're hungry again?
...I'll see what I can do!

Or Dick Grayson's gymnastics skills.
Hi, Bruce!

koff
And some powers are downright embarrassing.
Like "Stinkbomb" Starkwell's toxic flatulence.
Gag!
WC
I'm gonna be sick!

But still, they're **powers.**
And without powers here, I'm a nobody.

I can't compete in track...
Lapped you *again,* slowpoke!
GOTHAM

And again!
GOTHAM

And again!
GOTHAM
GOTHAM

...or swimming...

...or history...
Lex, this is the most amazing history essay I've ever read.
Your thesis on the need of the proletariat to topple the ruling classes was just exquisite.

...or French...
Très magnifique, Brainiac!
I have never had a student master French in just two days before!

...or science.
Wonderful work with your botany project, Pamela!

...or math.

Psst! Bruce! Let me see your answers!
No, Clark! Do your own work!

Hey! Stop using your X-ray vision to see my answers! That's cheating!

What are you gonna do about it? Tell the teacher?
Maybe.

Hey, everyone! Bruce is wearing undies with cartoon bunny rabbits on them!

HA HA HA
HA HA!
I can't possibly compete against everyone else here.
HA HA HA
HA HA!

I'm a wimp.
A loser.

They're all so much cooler than me.
So much more powerful.
And yet, the most terrifying, intimidating person at school isn't a student. It's...

Bruce Wayne! The vice principal wants to see you in his office!
GULP
The vice principal wants to see me???
Oooh! You're in trouble!
Nice knowing you, Bruce!

"Bruce, as a rule, I don't like to pull children out of class. But in this situation, I felt I had to make an exception.
SCHOOL PSYCHIATRIST
DR. CRANE

As you may recall, a few days ago, we had all the students here fill out self-evaluations so we could get an idea of your psychological states.

I have them right here. I've been reviewing them all.
Of particular interest was what everyone here would like to do for a living.

For example, Clark Kent would like to be a professional football player. While Arthur Curry would like to be a marine biologist.
Diana Prince would like to be a rodeo star. Selina Kyle would like to be a veterinarian who specializes in cats.
All good, wholesome professions...

And then there's *your* answer.
Name:
BRUCE WAYNE
What career do you imagine for yourself?
VIGILANTE

Needless to say, this has caused a great deal of consternation amongst the administration here.
"Vigilante" is not a profession, Bruce. It is a person who acts outside the bounds of legal authority.

I didn't mean to upset anyone! In fact, I just want to help people!
I want to do good!
To fight for truth and justice!
To avenge the loss of my parents by ridding Gotham of crime!

How do *you* expect to fight crime? Look at yourself!
You're a wimp with no powers!

I know, but...maybe I can find a way. Maybe I could be one of the great crime-fighters of the city...

...like Commissioner Gordon!

Commissioner Gordon is a police officer! He doesn't fight crime on his own!

Gotham Prep does not endorse vigilantism. It is dangerous!
What do you think would happen if I encouraged a student like Clark Kent to fight crime?
Well, he *is* bulletproof. So it wouldn't be *that* dangerous...

Bruce, I want you to forget about this misguided idea. In fact, I never want to hear about it again.
You'll only get yourself in trouble. Why don't you pick a career you would actually be good at?
Like philanthropy?

Philanthropy? But that doesn't require any skill at all.
Exactly! It's perfect for you!
Plus, you're the richest person in Gotham.

Speaking of philanthropy, I could use a new coffee maker in my office.

You're asking for me to buy you a new coffee maker? After my parents paid for this whole school?
I'm not asking you for anything. I'm just saying it might be a nice gesture on your part.
Perhaps as thanks for keeping you out of detention.

Detention? What did I do to get detention?
I heard you were cheating in math class.
Clark Kent was cheating! Not me! He looked right through my body!
You're blaming this on Clark? He won't like that...Now you're going to have detention—and the strongest kid in the school angry with you. Unless...

I'll have Alfred pick out a nice new coffee maker today.
That's very kind of you, Bruce.
Now why don't you run on back to class? I believe you have P.E. next?

P.E.?
Oh no. I forgot. Today I have...

DODGEBALL!
Not surprisingly, I'm always the last to get picked on a team for this.
GOTHAM
After that, I just try to make it out alive.
I mean, dodgeball was dangerous enough back at my old school...

WHAM
GOTHAM
But here, playing with kids with superpowers...
It's like being in a war.

So I have to do what I can to survive. Hiding behind other players is a good start...

Although that only works as long as there are other kids to hide behind.
BLAM
After that, I generally try to slip off the court and act like I was taken out before anyone notices me...

Hey, Bruce!

Looks like it's just down to you and me.

Here. I'll give you a fighting chance.
If you can take me out, you'll be a hero.
GOTHAM

You know that's not gonna happen. So why don't we just agree that you won and save me some pain?
Hey, everyone! Looks like Bruce has a secret power after all! He's part chicken!
GOTHAM

Are you chicken, Bruce? *Bock bock bock!*
Don't let him talk to you like that, Bruce. You can take him.

GOTHAM

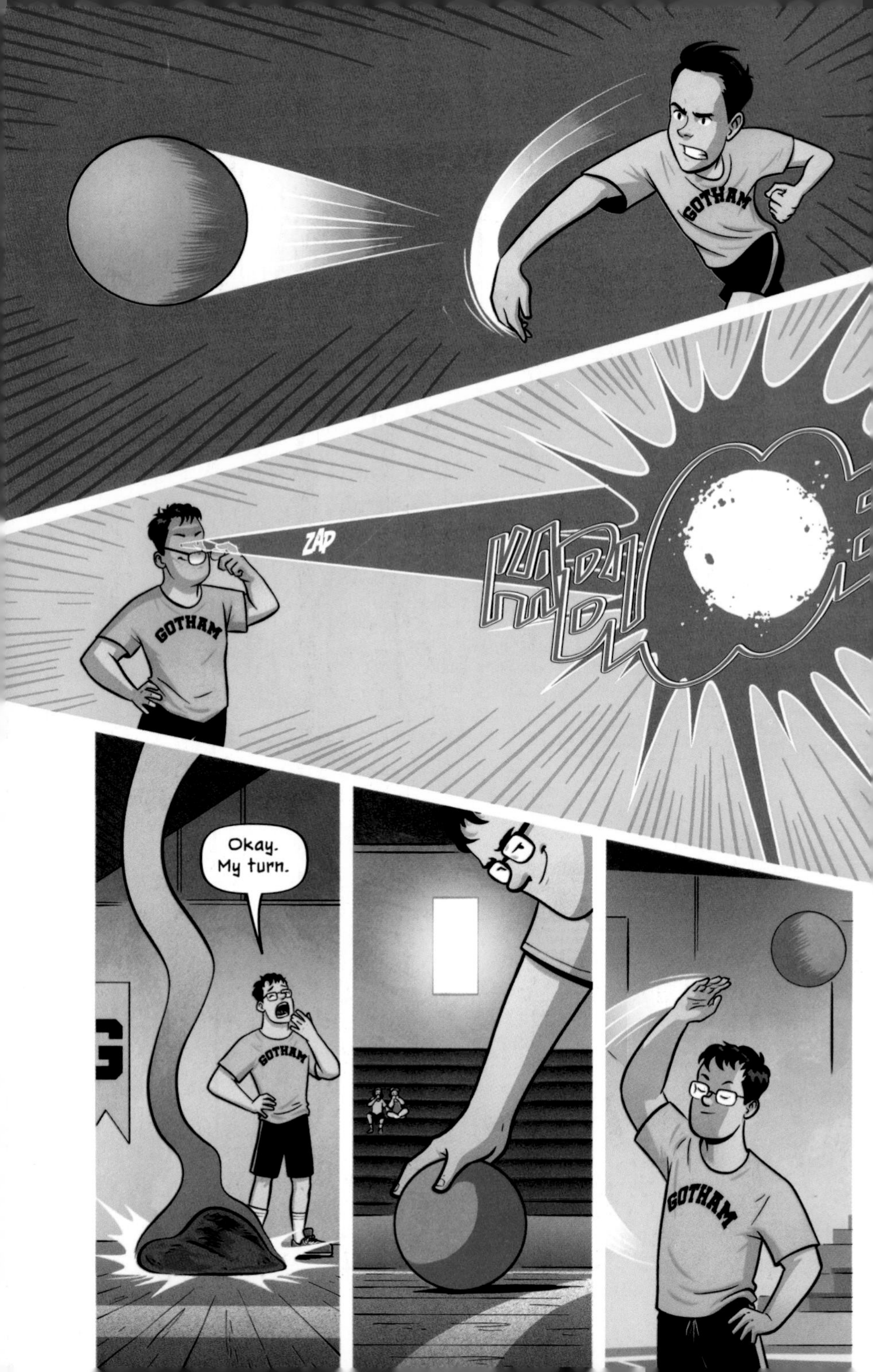
GOTHAM
GOTHAM
ZAP
Okay.
My turn.
GOTHAM
GOTHAM

WHAM

Unghhhhh—

KRASH

I can't believe I got in trouble for saying I want to be a vigilante.

I know, I know. I'm such a loser that my only friend is an 11-year-old in the elementary school at Gotham Prep.

But it's better than having no friends at all.

Even if Dick can't sit still for a second.

I mean, ***someone*** has to fight for justice in this city.

Except for Commissioner Gordon, the police are ineffectual...

And the politicians are all corrupt...

And honestly, why do we even have an asylum for dangerous villains right in the middle of our city?
That's just asking for trouble.
Gee whiz, Bruce, you're right.
ARKHAM ASYLUM

Sigh
I know I'm not the best person for the job.
It'd be far better if someone like Clark Kent fought crime—
—instead of me.

He's so strong and tough and cool. I don't stand a chance around him.
All the girls think he's awesome.
Diana Prince doesn't even look at me when he's around.

You like Diana Prince?
Everyone likes Diana Price. She's amazing.
I think you'd have a better chance with Selina Kyle.
Why's that?

Because she's been following us.

Hi, Bruce.
You know my name?

Of course I do.
Are you okay? I was worried you might be hurt after the dodgeball game today.

I'm fine. Are these all your cats?
No. Cats just like me. I have this weird connection with them.

Worst power ever, right?
It's better than not having any powers at all.
I guess.

It's kind of dangerous around here. Any chance you could walk me home?

Sure!
Well, here's my place!

Bye, Bruce! See you tomorrow!
Bye, Dick!
Which way's your house, Selina?

I didn't mean could you walk me to *my* home.
I meant could you walk me to *yours?*

Er... Really?
Yes!

I hear you live in the biggest mansion in Gotham! I'd love to see it!
Is it true that you have an indoor pool and a ballroom and a private bowling alley and 36 bedrooms?

Uh...no. That isn't true.

Oh.
Never mind then. See you around.

It actually has 38 bedrooms.
Sigh

Middle school stinks.

Chapter 2: The Worst Kid in Gotham

Bruce Wayne thinks middle school stinks?

That's a laugh.

He has Wayne Manor, the biggest house in Gotham.

He has a butler. He has everything anyone could ever want.
But me...?

I've got nothing.
MIRO'S GROCERY
My name's Jack.
Jack Napier.
HA
HA
HA

I go to Gotham Prep, too.
Although, unlike Moneybags Wayne, I couldn't buy my way in.
I had to fake my way in.

Gotham Prep admissions office. One year earlier.
So...Mr. Napier...you claim you can see ghosts?
I don't claim it. I can see them.
In fact, there's one behind you right now!
Where?
I don't see anything.
That's because you can't see ghosts.
Very few people can.
Except me.
PWANG

What was that?!

The ghost is getting angry. He wants to destroy your office.
If you'd like, I could tell him to calm down... because that's my superpower.
Although, if you still doubt me...I can just leave.

Should I tell the janitorial staff they'll need to be cleaning up in here?
Wait!
Please. Talk to the ghost.

GOTHAM PRE
ADMISSION
JACK NAPIER
ACCEPTED
KA-THUNK

While this swanky school is way better than the last place I attended, my life here still isn't easy.
JONES
88
At my old school, I was the toughest kid. I could shake down anyone for their lunch money...but in a school full of supers?
It's not so easy to find someone to pick on.
Hey, runt. Gimme all your money... or else.
Who are you calling a runt?
Eep.

SMASH
KLANG
Unghhh.
GOTHAM PREP ELEMENTARY SCHOOL
I have to stoop a lot lower to find a decent target.
Like this doofus.
Dick Grayson does his patented flipper-dipper...
...followed by the super-swirl...
...then the quadruple-wingnut...
...then the flying squirrel...

...and then sticks the landing! The crowd goes wild!
WHUMP
Oh. Hi.

Gimme all your money, loser!
Okay! Don't hurt me!
Here you go! This is everything I have!

Three bucks? That's all you've got?
Sorry!

Thanks for wasting my time, jerk.

Way to be a hero, Bruce.

Dick? Are you all right?
No. That mean kid took all my money...
I earned that fair and square walking my neighbor's dog.
I was gonna get myself an ice cream cone.

C'mon. Ice cream is on me.
Really? Gee, thanks, Bruce!

You're the best!

Three measly bucks. Where are all the good targets in this town?

Thanks for this. You're a good guy, Bruce.
No. I'm not.
Instead of letting Jack bully you, I should have stood up to him.
How? You don't have any powers. You're just...
...normal.
I know.
GKC 2403

This is what I'm talking about.

Easy money.
The thing is, crime is rampant in this city and ***no one*** is doing anything about it.

All the supers are just squandering their powers.
So I guess the hard work is up to normal folks like me.

The next time I see someone doing something wrong—
—I'm not going to just sit by and watch it happen...
WHOOSH
SHIVER

I'm going to ***act.***
All I need is a chance to stand up for what's right.

Gimme your money, kid!
Help! Help!
Any chance at all.
Like, maybe someone little and weak getting picked on by someone big and mean.

Someone please help me!
The moment something like that happens, I'll jump right in without a moment's hesitation.
Uh... Bruce?

Looks like there's some trouble right now.
Where?!

Yes! This is exactly what I'm talking about!
That little girl is being victimized! This is great!
Er... okay.

This is my moment!
Hey! Leave that little girl alone!
Back away from her, evildoer!
Oooh. You're in trouble!
Or I will dispense justice...

SCREECH
Jack?

Aaaaaaahhhhh!
SLIP

Oof!
WHAM
WHIRRRR
Aaaaaaaaaaaaaaaaah!
WHIZZZZZZZZZ

Aaaaaaaaaaaaaah!
Uh-oh...

My money! Hooray! You got it back!
I did what now?

Stay away from me! I already gave the money back!
Please don't hurt me!

Aaaaaaaaah!

You saved me! Who are you?
I'm...

...er...
GCPD

...well...

PARK RULES
1- NO DOGS
2- NO SMOKING
3- NO VIGILANTES

I'm just someone trying to make a difference.
I gotta go. Bye!

Are you all right, Donna?

Sure thing, big sis.
Thanks to that friendly vigilante.

What a good person.
I wonder who he is?

Chapter 3: The Birth of the Bat

Alfred!

Alfred! I thwarted evil today!

THWUP

SMACK

SMACK
You did what?!

THWUP
I chased off a bully who was terrorizing little kids! I was a vigilante!
SMACK
I want to do it more!
Come help me make a costume!

THWUP
A costume?!

SMACK

Bruce, all you did was stop one kid. And now you want to start fighting crime?

Why don't you do something more productive, like go out for the school chess team?

I don't want to play chess! I want to fight for truth, justice, and decency.

Even at my school, immorality is rampant. There are bad kids with powers who are probably going to be super-villains someday...
And I'm pretty sure that our school psychologist, Dr. Crane, is secretly evil.
Sigh...
Bruce, this is just another one of your silly phases...
Like when you decided you wanted to be a professional skateboarder. Only, this time, you could get hurt.
I got hurt plenty when I tried to be a professional skateboarder.
American History
True Crime
Oh. Right. Well, this time...you could get killed.
Not if I do this right. That's why I need your help.
Parenting
Give me one good reason why I should help you.
Uh...because it's your job?
Sigh. I suppose you're right.
Biology

So...what kind of costume were you thinking? Like a soldier? Or a knight? Or a samurai?
No. An animal.
An animal?!

A *dangerous* animal. One that will strike fear into the hearts of everyone who sees it!
Animals
Aha! Here we go!
Nature
SNATCH
The World's Scariest Animals

FLIP FLIP FLIP
Here we go! This is what I need to look like!
It's perfect!

Rats.
This doesn't
look nearly as
intimidating as
I'd hoped.
Back to
the drawing
board?

Too bulky.
Ah-choo!
I think I'm allergic to this fur.
Sniffle
Sniffle
HONEYBADGER
TIGER!!
I don't have any arms!
Now I have too many arms!

Sigh
This is harder than I thought.
Bruce, I think you're going about this all wrong.
This animal thing is a mistake.

Personally, I don't find animals the slightest bit scary.
There's nothing remotely frightening about them at all.
FLAP
FLAP
FLAP
FLAP

FLAP
FLAP
FLAP
FLAP
A bat! Aaugh!
Get it away from me! *Get it away!*
PANDA-MAN!

With this new vigilante in town, I need to step up my game.
It's no longer safe for me to shake kids down for their money one at a time.
Instead, I need to steal everyone's money all at once.
I admit, it's not the crime of the century, but that will come later.
For now, I'll settle for the crime of the semester.
But in order to contend with this new nemesis of mine, I'll need some muscle...
That's where you come in, Bane.
So what do you say? Want to make some extra cash?

This looks great!

Intimidating, yet functional.

Imposing, yet comfy.

And it works thematically with my secret lair.

What do you think? I'm going to call it...
The Batcave!
This has been down here the whole time?
Why would your family build a mansion over a cave?
And why would they put an elevator down into it?

We'll put the weapons shop over by that dangerous crevice...
And we'll put the martial arts training arena by that enormous pile of bat guano!
Urk...

Oh! There's also a secret entrance big enough to drive a car through that's conveniently concealed by a massive waterfall.
So I could get a Batmobile and trick it out with all sorts of cool weapons!

What's a Batmobile?
A car designed to kind of look like a bat. But with cannons and stuff.
No. You're too young to drive.
Okay. I could get a Bat-bicycle and trick it out with all sorts of weapons.
You're not putting weapons on any sort of vehicle.
*Er...*I could get a bicycle and put some cool stickers on my helmet.
I suppose.
You know, I should probably learn how to fight.
Seeing as I'll be confronting evil on a regular basis.
Sigh
Good idea.
I'll go start the training montage music.

BAT-BOLAS!
BAT-LASSO
Jeez... Diana Prince always makes this look so easy.

BAT-- TASER
Aaaaaaaah!
ZZZZZZAP
BAT-HOOK
KRAK
KRASH
Look out!

BAT-
BAT?
Bruce!
Sorry!
WHOOOSH
BAT
CHLOROFORM
Ahh...
Ahhh...
AH-
CHOO!
Sigh
THUD

BATARANG
WHOOSH
Hey! I did it! I actually did something well!
Er... Bruce...I just realized...
When you throw a boomerang well... it comes *back* to you.
WHIZZZ
AAAAAAAAH!!!
Okay, I've tried the Bat-Bolos, the batarang, the Bat-Lasso, the Bat-Shark Repellent, the Bat-Mace, the Bat-Lance, the Bat-Taser, the Bat-Brass Knuckles, the Bat-Bat, the Bat-Catapult, the Bat-Chloroform, the Bat-Bombs...
Might I suggest the Bat-tub next?
Bat-tub?

Oh.

And use soap, Bruce!

After all that working out in a guano-filled cave, you stink.

Meanwhile, at Gotham City Park.
HEE HEE HEE HEE

HA HA HA HA

We'll pull off the heist during the homecoming football game tonight.

No one ever wants to miss that game...

So all the students and faculty will be in the stands.

While they're all distracted, we'll break into every-one's lockers at once...
And rob them all blind!

HA HA HA
HA HA
And what do I do?

Keep an eye out for that goody-two-shoes vigilante. And if he tries to stop us...
Hurt him.
Oooh. Good plan.

Jinkies! I need to warn Bruce!

PANT
PANT
PANT
Gasp!
I should have just called him. This driveway must be a mile long!

Hello?
Hi! I'm Bruce's friend, Dick Grayson!
I need to talk to Bruce right away! It's an emergency!

...and then Jack's going to rob everyone's lockers all at once!
It's the crime of the semester!
This sounds like a job for... the Caped Crusader!
Who?

To the Batcave!
Where?
I feel like I missed some exposition...

Wow! This is amazing!
And check this out!

Ta-da!
Whoa! That's a great badger costume!

Dude, I'm a bat.
Really?
Why would I be dressed as a badger in a Batcave?

Er...because badgers eat bats?
Sigh
No. They don't.

Well, it's still a really awesome costume.
I don't suppose you have one for me, too?

Why would *you* need a costume?
So I could fight crime alongside you!
You mean like...as a sidekick?

Well...I'm not that good at predicting the future, but sure!
Not "psychic." ***Sidekick!***
Oh! That makes much more sense!

I could dress in red and yellow and have a really scary animal name...
...like Robin!

Um...robins aren't scary.
Like heck they're not!
When I was little, one pecked me with its beak. ***Hard.*** They're terrifying.

Imagine us! Batman and Robin!
The Dynamic Duo!
I didn't make any extra costumes.

So...next time?
Er...yeah. Maybe.
I better get going.

Oh! I almost forgot!
Jack is working with Bane on this.

Bane?!
And just who is this Bane person?
Er...he's just a kid from school.
A kid with super-strength and brains who concocted his own steroid system in chemistry class!
He's really dangerous.

Then you're staying home, Bruce.
Nice going.

Neat-o!
WHOOSH
There's no way you're fighting that kid.
He'll kill you.

I'm not going to fight him!
Or at least, I'm going to try very hard not to.
I don't want to get hurt.

WHOOSH
But I can't just sit still and let Jack rob everyone in the school.
Why not? Those other kids don't care about *you.* They don't treat you nicely.

CLONK
Ow!
Clark Kent routinely uses his X-ray vision to see what kind of underwear you have on and then tells all the girls about it.
You don't owe those kids anything.

So I'm taking you back upstairs. Where it's safe.

Safe?!
What kind of hero worries about their own safety?
PING

If I turn my back now and let Jack get away with this crime...then it will only lead to Jack wanting more.
Jack will never learn that crime doesn't pay.

Which will encourage him to commit bigger and bigger crimes.
Until, maybe, he becomes the most devious, dangerous super-villain in Gotham City history...

A diabolical criminal who will stop at nothing to cause chaos, mayhem, and anarchy!

Well, I'm not gonna let that happen!

A hero can't only confront evil when it's safe.
A true hero must take risks.
If we don't, then society as we know it will crumble.

That was a very moving speech, Bruce.
But you're still not going.
PING

I admit, this job is cushy. You're not that much work.
I make you mac and cheese, drive you to school, play video games with you...and in return, I get to live in the biggest, fanciest house in Gotham.
But I *did* swear to your parents that I would take care of you.
I thought this whole vigilante thing was just a phase and that you'd get bored of it...
The same way you're bored of all these other things.
But you haven't quit. Which is kind of admirable.
And yet, I still can't let you go up against this Bane guy. He has super-strength and you...
You're just normal.

I'm still going after Jack! And you can't stop me!
Actually, I can.

You're grounded.
Let me out!
No. You're staying in there until you realize that vigilantism is nothing but trouble!

Come on, Dick. I'll drive you home.
This is so uncool!
I'll bet Commissioner Gordon never gets grounded.

Chapter 4: The Dark Night of the Dark Knight

Soon, everyone will be in the stands.
Once the game starts, the school will be empty...
1st

And we'll be free to put our plan into action.

I don't care if I get in trouble with Alfred.
I don't care if Bane is Jack's muscle.

I don't care if I have no superpowers.
I can't sit here and do nothing while the crime of the semester is being committed.

I'm going to stop Jack!

Gulp.

What kind of hero would I be if I let fear of plummeting to my death stop me from doing good?

Aaaaaaah!!

Help! Help me!

No! Help me!

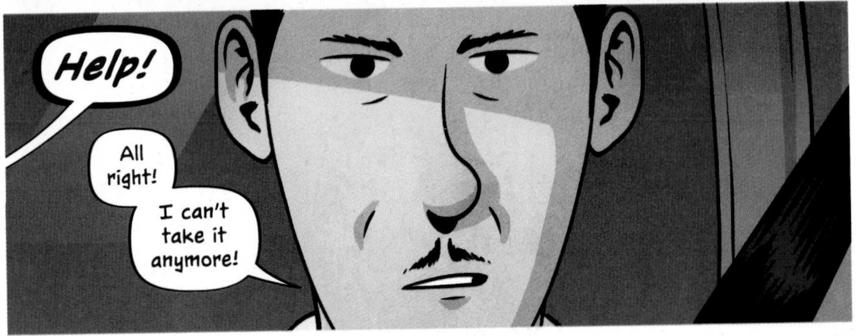

SCREECH

Stop! Leave that poor woman alone, you big jerk!

Poor woman?
She's mugging *me!*

You'll never catch me alive!
Thank you!
CLANK

It's about time *someone* tried to make a difference in this town.
*Er...*You're welcome.

What's wrong?
I just saved that poor innocent thug.
And you're not happy about that?

Bruce was right.
VROOM

All these people just need someone to stand up for them.
They need a little hope.

SCREEEEEEECH

Sorry, Dick. But we need to get back to Wayne Manor.
I was wrong to ground Bruce.

VROOM

So...You're going to let Bruce be a vigilante?
Of course not! There's no way I am doing that!

But I can still be a little more supportive.

Oof.

The football game has already begun! I have to gear up!
8:15PM

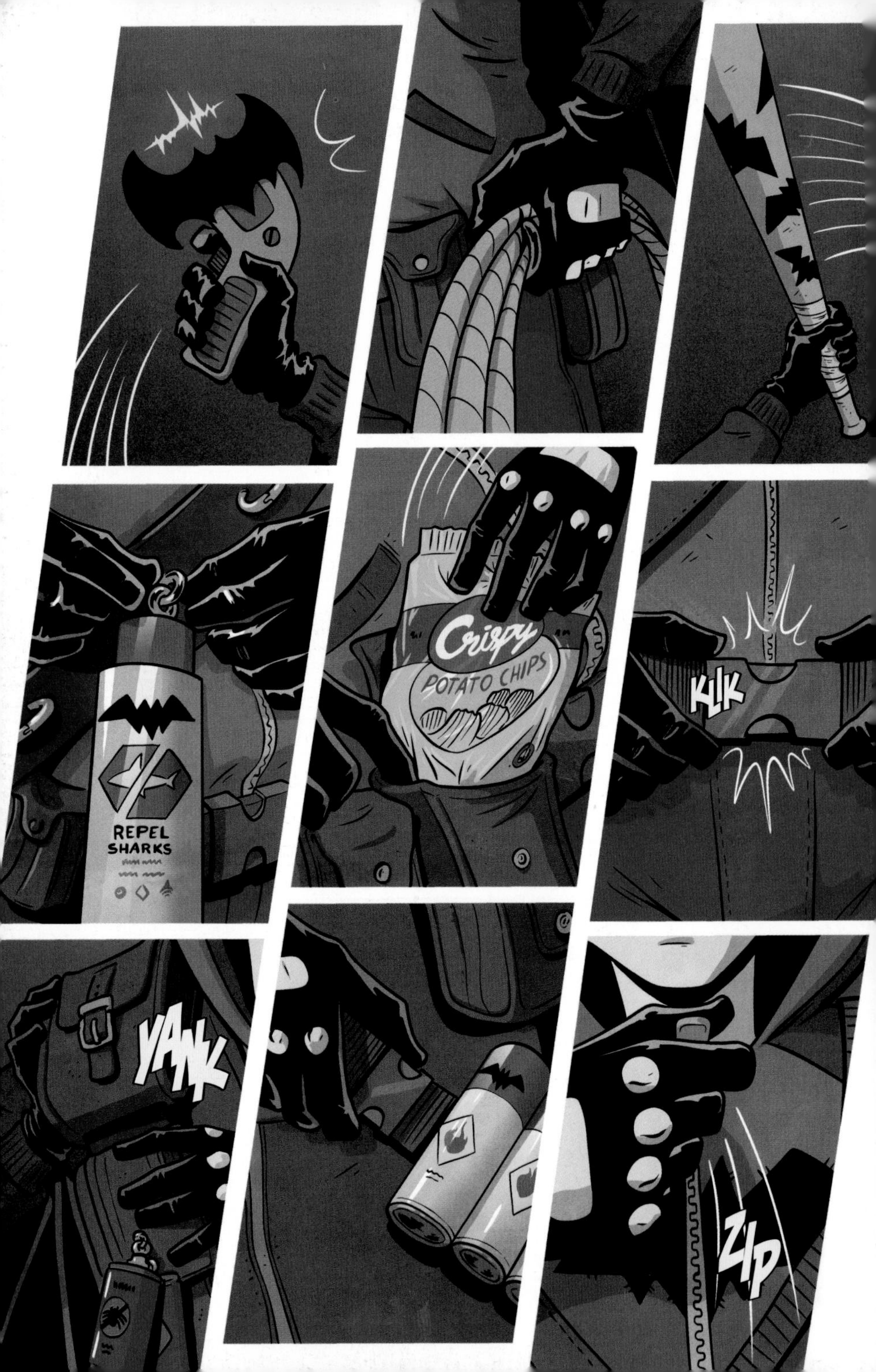
Crispy
POTATO CHIPS
REPEL
SHARKS
KLIK
YANK
ZIP

Hmmmm.
I probably ought to leave some of this at home.
8:30PM
KLANG

Meanwhile, at Gotham Prep, the game is underway.
Blue 42! Blue 42! Hut! Hut!
Hike!
SHOVE
Clark! I'm open!
ZOOOOOOOM
SNAP

I got it!
GOTHAM
Touchdown!
Ooof!
HOORAY! GO GOTHAM!
GOTHAM PREP
METROPOLIS MIDDLE SCHOOL
QTR 1
48
13:00
00
KLIK
I don't know why we even come to these games. They're never even close.
We're up 48-zip and we've only been playing two minutes.
CLARK!
Hey, Diana...
CLARK!
GOTHAM
#1
CLARK!
CLARK!

Diana, I gotta go pee.
So go. There are bathrooms right over there.
I can't use those...
"Stinkbomb Starkwell just went in there."

I need to use the bathrooms in the school.
Oh, all right.
I'll come with you...

Another touchdown for Gotham!
HOORAY!
This game stinks.

Where'd he go?
Maybe we should check the Batcave?

He's not here either!
But he's taken some of his supplies.
And his Bat-Bicycle is gone!

He must have gone to confront Jack and Bane!
Come on! We've got to find him and stop him before he gets into trouble!

Every other butler I know just has to make tea and sandwiches.
But I've got to keep my master from getting himself killed.

Check this out!
It's a heat ray I built in my garage!
How's it work?
Just watch!
WHIP
HA HA HA HA HA
SIZZLE
SIZZLE
BZZZZZZZTTTT
It works!
Everyone's stuff is now *our* stuff!
HA HA HA HA HA
MATH

WHOA!
Sounds like something exciting actually happened.
I gotta go so bad!

Just go on in by yourself.
I want to see what happened at the game.
I don't want to go by myself!
What if it's dangerous?

It's just my school! It's not dangerous.
I promise, nothing's gonna happen to you.

GASP!

Bane!
Grab her!
MMmmMMM!
SLAP
What do I do with her?
Get rid of her!
We can't have any witnesses!
Let the girl go!

SMASH

I said, let the girl...
AAAAAAAAGH!
It's Weasel Boy!
THUMP
Weasel Boy? Really?
Weasels don't have wings.
Flying weasels do.
There's no such thing as a flying weasel!
I'm a bat!
You look more like a muskrat to me.
Actually, I think he looks like a prairie dog...

I'm a bat! A really scary bat!
I'M BATMAN!!!
Now put down the girl and hand over your ill-gotten booty!
You said *booty*.
Bane, put down the girl...
And clobber the bat.
You want to play rough?
Okay. Let's play rough.
BOOM
BOOM
BOOM
SNATCH
KLIK

FLOP
Whoops!
WHOOSH
WHIRRRR
TRIP
Uh-oh...

GACK!
THWACK

That was some rescue.
Gimme a break.
It's my first day with the new costume... URK!

Not such a big hero now, are you?
Bane, take this loser's mask off so we can see who he *really* is.

Then let's hang him by his undies from the flagpole...
To send a lesson to all the other students that being a hero doesn't pay.
HA HA HA HA HA

Chapter 5: Super After All

CHEMISTRY LABORATORY
I'll admit, this wasn't working out quite the way I had hoped.

No one knew where I was.
I was powerless against Bane.
And I obviously wasn't very good with my weapons yet.
Plus, I had no pants.
You've made a big mistake coming here, Badger Boy.
You're in way over your head.
I mean, it's obvious you don't have any superpowers at all.
But in that very moment, I realized that Jack was wrong.
And I had been wrong, too.
Wait!

I *did* have a power.
I was **smart**.
And being smart might just be the greatest power that there is.
You guys are making a big mistake.

You're the one making the mistake here.
Trying to be a hero was a bad career move.

Yeah? I'm not the one missing the big score.

I'll check for him outside!
I'll look inside the school!
Is something wrong?
My little sister is in there!

What do you mean, we're missing the big score?
You're going through all this trouble just to steal from the lockers?
All you're getting is spare change and dirty gym shorts.
A *smart* person would hit the chemistry lab.
That's where they keep all the expensive stuff.
Like what kind of stuff?
Precious metals. Expensive chemicals.
The stuff in there is worth thousands of dollars.
They keep it locked in a secret safe.
Where is it?
I'll have to show you.

SUPPLY CLOSET
There! That's where they keep the good stuff!
That just looks like a normal supply closet.
It doesn't look like they'd keep anything expensive in there at all.
GAS
Well, it wouldn't be very smart of them to store everything in a closet marked "really expensive stuff," would it?
HISSSSSSSSSS

By the way, that isn't a normal door.
It's actually super-strong.
So you're going to need your heat ray to get through it.
And then we can all split the proceeds three ways.
Three ways?
I don't think so, Badger Boy.
You didn't do anything to help.
I told you what to steal!
I'm the ***brains*** of this operation!
I'm the brains! Not you!
Bane, get him out of here.
HA-HA HA HA
Are you okay?
THUD

I am, thanks.
But we have to get out of here...
NOW!

Bruce! Where are you going?

Dick?!
Get out of the building!

We're about to be rich!
HA HA HA HA
SUPPLY CLOSET
HISSSSSSS
GAS
WHOOSH

KA-BOO

WHOOSH
CRUMBLE
CRUMBLE
YIKES!
ZIP
SMASH
YANK

METROPOLIS MIDDLE SCHOOL
BOOM
GASP
GASP
FLING
KENT
10
JONES
Our school is on fire!
WOO HOO!
Our school is on fire!
WOO HOO!
WOO HOO!
WOO HOO!

Curse that badger!
He foiled my plans!
...I want a pony...

What happened back there?
I tricked those hooligans into defeating themselves!

You see, I realized something important.
I *do* have a superpower. My mind!

In fact, being smart isn't just the best power we have...
It's a power that *anyone* can have.
You just have to try.

Hmmmm.

It's still not as cool as super-strength.
Or flying.
Or being able to telepathically communicate with kittens.
Sigh.

Donna! You're all right!

Your big sister was so worried!
Thanks for saving her, Ferret Boy.

Er...I'm actually a bat.
But I have wings!
Really? You look like a ferret.
Oh. I thought those were supposed to be skin flaps of some sort.

Skin flaps?
Anyhow, you're still a hero.
And this city *needs* a hero.

SMOOCH

Are you all right?
Yes...
Thanks to you?
What's with the getup?
Are you going to a costume party?
No! I'm the sidekick to a hero! I'm...

FLUTTER
FLUTTER
ROBIN!
TWEET
That's not a very imposing name for a sidekick...
No! There's a robin right behind you!
Run for your life!

Aaaaaaaaaaaaaah!
Donna! You're all right!
Yeah! A boy dressed as a muskrat saved me!

Y'know, I saved someone, too.
Really?
Wow, big sis!
That's super-cool!
Actually... it *was.*

Should you ever need a hero again, just use this.
What is it?
It's a Bat-Signal.
You put it over a flashlight—or a big spotlight, if you have one handy—and shine it up into the clouds.
And when I see it, I'll come as fast as I can.
Er...How is this supposed to work if it's daytime?
Or if there aren't any clouds?
Oh... Well...It's really just a prototype.
I'm still figuring things out.

What happened?
My goodness!
I'd better go.
But I still don't know how to find you again!
Don't worry!
I'll be around!

Who was that?
Ferret Dude.
Batman!
GOTHAM
10
GOTHAM

He saved my sister...
And thwarted the crime of the semester!
I don't think he had any.
Really? With what kind of powers?
KEN

No powers?
How could anyone fight crime without any powers?
He found a way.
Just think about it...
If he could fight crime *without* any powers... imagine what all of us could do *with* our powers.
Maybe, instead of using our powers for our own benefit, we could use them to help other people.
We could form some sort of League of Justice and help make this city safe again!
GOTHAM
10
GOTHAM
I'd rather be a pro football player.
Or an Olympic athlete.
Or a marine biologist.
Sigh.
GOTHAM
10
GOTHAM
23
I'm going to join the Air Force.
I'm going into professional archery.
I want to work with penguins.
I think you'd make a cool hero, big sis.
Thanks, kiddo.
There was something *familiar* about that ferret...
JONES
88

Want a lift?
Yeah. It's been a big night.
WAYNE

The horror. The horror.
SHIVER
SHIVER

Poor Dick!
He must have really been shaken up by that explosion.
Er...no. He saw a robin.
Oh.
I guess I'm in big trouble for being a vigilante?
Actually... no.

Your heart is in the right place, Bruce.
It's good to want to make a difference.
It's a good thing to want to help people.

I'm just concerned that you'll get hurt.
So maybe, instead of just telling you not to try...

I could help you do things more safely.
That would be great!

This is Gotham.
It might be dangerous and polluted and have a really decrepit public transportation system...
But it's still my city.

I have sworn an oath to take care of it.
To keep its citizens safe.

I am vengeance.

I am virtue.

I am Batman.

I am...

Bruce! Get off the roof before you fall and break your neck!

...up way past my bedtime.

Give me a break. I'm just a kid.

It's going to take a while until I get this superhero thing figured out.

Boys,
I am very disappointed in you.
Yeah. We broke the rules and destroyed the school.
No.
You didn't think big enough.
You went to all the trouble to invent a heat ray like that...
And you used it to rob your *school?*
With tech like that, you should have gone after a bank.
Or a gold depository.
Plus, you allowed yourself to get tricked by a kid dressed as a flying rat.
Next time, that's not going to happen.
Next time?
But we're supposed to go to juvenile hall for our crimes...
Not if I step in.

The juvenile hall system is totally corrupt.
I can fix it so that you stay at this school.
I mean, I'm the one who got you in here in the first place.
You? No. I conned my way in!
With that silly seeing ghosts thing? Please.
You're here because of me.
I've been looking for someone like you.
VICE PRINCIPAL HUGO STRANGE
I have plenty of ideas for what kids with your strength and lack of morals can do.
And what about the flying badger?
Don't worry about the rodent.
I know exactly how to handle him.
Hahaha.
Hahaha!

HA HA HA HA HA HA HA HA HA

Stay tuned for the further
adventures of Badger Boy
...er, Batman!

PHOTO CREDIT: DASHIELL GIBBS

Stuart Gibbs is the author of five *New York Times* bestselling series: Spy School, FunJungle, Charlie Thorne, Moon Base Alpha, and Once Upon a Tim. He has also written for TV and film and researched capybaras, the world's largest rodents. (Really.) He lives with his family in Los Angeles.

Berat Pekmezci was born and grew up in Istanbul, where he first began his studies in graphic arts. With a keen interest in storytelling and visual narrative, he turned his talents toward illustration and published his first graphic novels in Turkey. After working as an art director in advertising agencies for several years, he moved to London and has been illustrating book covers and children's books ever since. Berat enjoys doodling in his sketchbooks in his travels and spending time with his cat.

Check out this special sneak peek of

Clark & Lex

Being the only kid with powers is tough... and not being able to use them is even worse!

Struggling with understanding why his parents demand he hide his amazing superpowers, Clark has no problem using a bit of super-speed or super-strength to give himself that extra edge as quarterback of the football team or while doing his chores around the farm.

And when LuthorCorp holds a competition to find the best and brightest for a summer internship in Metropolis, he has no problem using his X-ray vision to cheat his way in if it means getting out of Smallville. Amazingly, Clark is not the only competitor with special abilities...just ask his newfound friend, Lex Luthor.

But as the kids go missing one by one, the boys realize the competition may not be all it seems. Can Clark put aside his pride for the sake of the team and become the friend and leader they will need to overcome LuthorCorp's ambitions?

Available Summer 2023!

I have an announcement. A special event will be taking place this week at Smallville Middle School.

A nationwide exam will be conducted here at school. Top scorers may earn the chance to compete for a truly remarkable grand prize.
BRAINWAVE

What could this be? Nothing cool ever happens in Smallville.

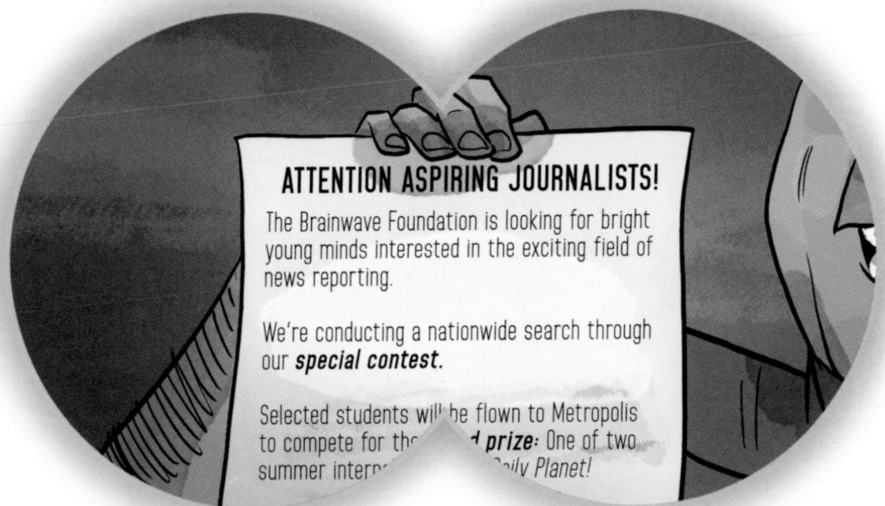
ATTENTION ASPIRING JOURNALISTS!
The Brainwave Foundation is looking for bright young minds interested in the exciting field of news reporting.
We're conducting a nationwide search through our ***special contest***.
Selected students wil
be flown to Metropolis
to compete for th
d prize: One of two
summer intern
aily Planet!

A written test will be administered during the last hour of school on Wednesday afternoon. Everyone is eligible to participate, but there's no requirement to do so.

If you think this all sounds strange, well...that's because it is. I've never heard of the like before.

Just do your best, but don't get your hopes up. There's no guarantee that anyone from Smallville will be selected.

BRAINWAVE

ATTENTION ASPIRING JOURNALISTS!

The Brainwave Foundation is looking for bright young minds interested in the exciting field of news reporting.

We're conducting a nationwide search through our **special contest**.

Selected students will be flown to Metropolis to compete for the **grand prize**: One of two summer internships at the Daily Planet!

Okay class, open your textbooks to the section on chlorophyll byproducts...
Man, a whole summer in Metropolis!

Imagine! Three months in the center of everything.

Otherwise, I'll be stuck here shucking corn. This is my chance to get away!

RRRIINNGGG

I have to do whatever it takes to win this contest.

BRAINWAVE
Wow.
Talk about overkill.

Can you believe this? It's *wild.* When did they put all these posters up?
No idea.
It's a little... creepy.

Creepy? I think you mean ***amazing!*** I could win an internship at the *Daily Planet!* My dream come true!
I wonder what the exam will cover?

Could be anything. Ms. Jordan said they're not telling anyone beforehand, not even our teachers. But the finals take place inside LuthorCorp Tower!
Seriously? Very cool.
I've been to the observation deck! It's so high I almost threw up.

I was ***born*** to win this contest. Mark it down— I'm going to Metropolis!
You're perfect for it, Eliza. Good luck!

*Not so fast. If they only take one winner from Smallville, it's going to be **me.** This is my ticket out of here!*
*And name something I **haven't** won lately.*

Heavens, Clark! Slow down. What's got you so worked up?

Mom, it's incredible! There's a contest at school, and the winners get a free trip to Metropolis. The grand prize is an internship for the whole summer!

I NEED A NEW LIFE!

TWO DAYS LATER AT LUNCHTIME...
Test day! I should snag some pizza and carbo-load before we start.
LIBRARY

Who are those people? They must all shop at the same website.

A little eavesdropping never hurt anyone...

Huh?

Yikes. None of my business...

RRRRIIIINNNGGGG

Pssst... Keith! Who's that guy up there?
How should I know?

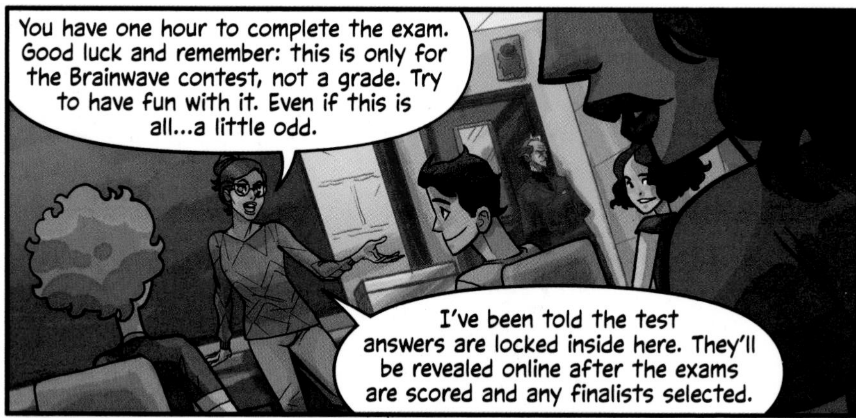
You have one hour to complete the exam. Good luck and remember: this is only for the Brainwave contest, not a grade. Try to have fun with it. Even if this is all...a little odd.
I've been told the test answers are locked inside here. They'll be revealed online after the exams are scored and any finalists selected.

Here we go! Time to ace this thing.

Whoa. What the heck is this?

You've got to be kidding me.

Just concentrate! I can do this. If the train is moving at 110 miles per hour...

Aha! Gotcha. It's **definitely** C.

Huh?! This second one is even worse than the first!

CORP
So the answers are in there, are they?
So easy... No one would ever know...

Too easy. Don't mind if I do!
Lead
. 12=X
. 75
. light
. Multiverse
. Siegle
Cheating with my powers? Dad would **kill** me if he knew.
He'd tell me to blend in like always. Fail this exam and do nothing. Well, I'm sick of it. Sick of being told not to be the best.

Besides, it's not cheating if they put the answers right there for me to see.

Annnnnd...done!

Metropolis, here I come!

!!!

Relax, Clark. He can't know a thing. Just play it cool and act natural.

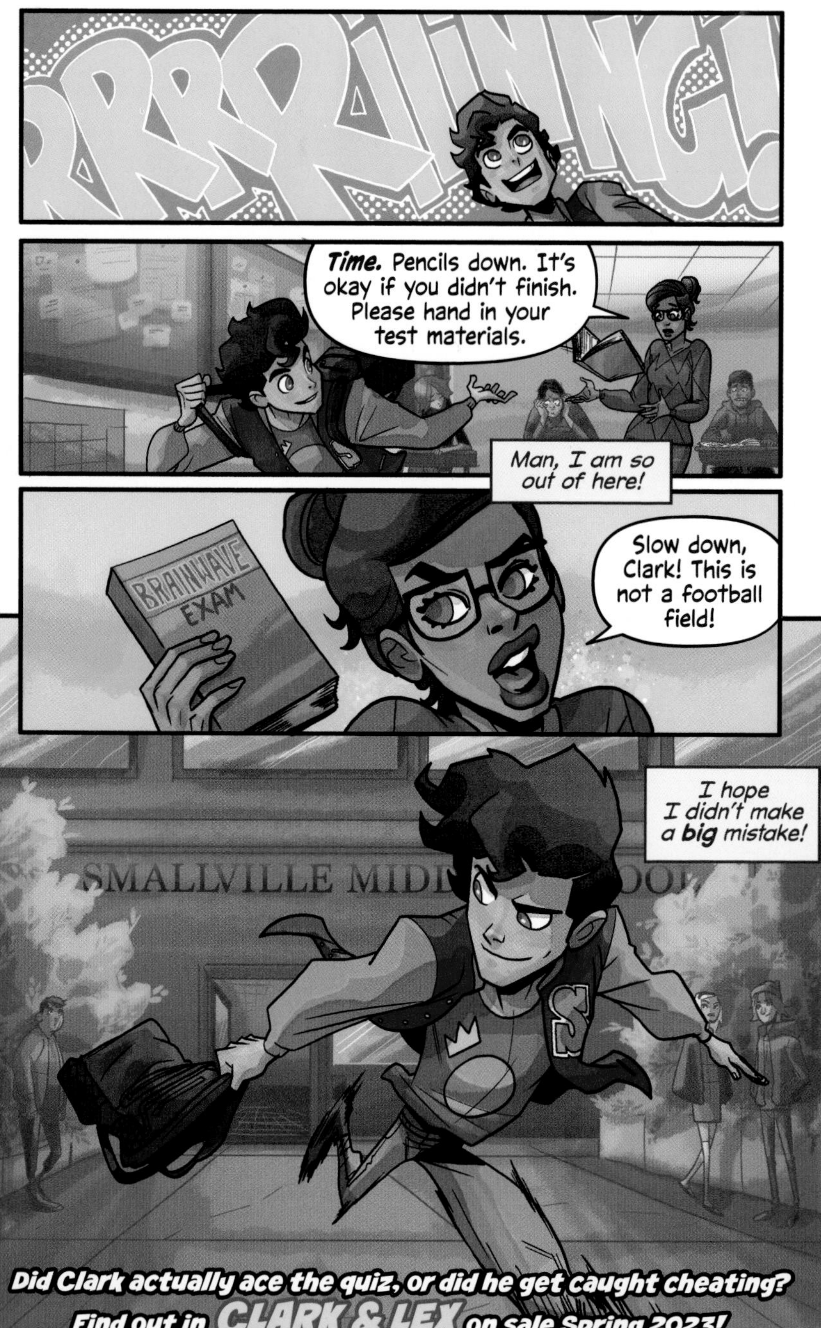
BRRRRIIINNG!
Time. Pencils down. It's okay if you didn't finish. Please hand in your test materials.
Man, I am so out of here!
BRAINWAVE EXAM
Slow down, Clark! This is not a football field!
I hope I didn't make a big mistake!
SMALLVILLE MIDD
Did Clark actually ace the quiz, or did he get caught cheating?
Find out in CLARK & LEX on sale Spring 2023!

MORE DC BOOKS FOR YOUNG READERS!

Dear Justice League
Michael Northrop, Gustavo Duarte
ISBN: 978-1-4012-8413-8
The greatest heroes in the DC Universe, the Justice League, answer mail from their biggest fans—kids!

Dear DC Super-Villains
Michael Northrop, Gustavo Duarte
ISBN: 978-1-77950-054-0
Peek inside the lives of DC's infamous rogues gallery in the sequel to *Dear Justice League*, where curious kids write to notorious scoundrels about life on the dark sdie.

Batman and Robin and Howard
Jeffrey Brown
ISBN: 978-1-4012-9768-8
Sidelined by a crime-fighting field trip gone wrong, Damian Wayne must refocus his attention on his life as an average student and learning how to be a team player—especially when he meets his match in his new rival, Howard.

My Buddy, Killer Croc
Sara Farizan, Nicoletta Baldari
ISBN: 978-1-77950-124-0
Andy is new to Gotham. He's shy and quiet and in need of friends. Then he meets his wrestling hero, Waylon Jones, now known as Killer Croc. How will Andy react when he finds out the truth about his idol?